An I Can Read Book®

Zack's Alligator Goes to School

story by Shirley Mozelle
pictures by James Watts

HarperTrophy®
A Division of HarperCollins*Publishers*

Zack's Alligator Goes to School

For information address HarperCollins Children's Books,
a division of HarperCollins Publishers,
195 Broadway, New York, NY 10007.

Library of Congress Cataloging-in-Publication Data
Mozelle, Shirley.
Zack's alligator goes to school / story by Shirley Mozelle ;
pictures by James Watts.
p. cm. — (An I can read book)
Summary: Bridget, an alligator key chain that grows into a full-sized creature when dunked in water, creates chaotic fun when Zack takes her to school for show-and-tell. Sequel to "Zack's Alligator."
ISBN 0-06-022887-3. — ISBN 0-06-022888-1 (lib. bdg.)
ISBN 0-06-444248-9 (pbk.)
[1. Alligators—Fiction. 2. Schools—Fiction.] I. Watts, James, date, ill. II. Title. III. Series.
PZ7.M868Za 1994 92-29871
[E]—dc20 CIP
AC

First Harper Trophy edition, 1998
16 SCP 30 29 28 27 26 25 24
❖
Visit us on the World Wide Web!
http://www.harperchildrens.com

For Bonnie Westmoe—
and Sally, Sheri, Nancy, and Nina
—S.M.

For Annabelle, Stuart, and Genevieve
—J.K.M.W.

Zack rode the school bus
with his best friend, Turk.
“Did you bring Bridget
for show-and-tell?”
asked Turk.

“Yes,” said Zack.

“She is here in my pocket.”

"You brought a *girl*
for show-and-tell?"
asked Buster.

"A girl *alligator*," said Zack.

"And she grows," said Turk.

"Sure," said Buster.

"What does she grow? Roses?"

Buster laughed.

"You will see," said Turk.

Buster reached into the big box

on his lap.

“This is *my* show-and-tell,”

he said.

“Negatron is the greatest robot

in the whole world.

He can do amazing things.”

“So can Bridget,” said Zack.

When they got to school,

everyone ran to class.

“Show-and-tell will begin,”

said Ms. Pickles.

“Let me go first,” said Buster.

“Go ahead, Buster,” said Ms. Pickles.

“This is Negatron!” said Buster.

Negatron can walk, run,

and shoot colored beams

from his ray pack. Watch!”

Click, buzzz, click, click.

Negatron did not work.

"It is probably just a loose screw,"

Buster said.

Everybody laughed.

"Maybe it needs new batteries,"

said Ms. Pickles.

Buster sat down.

“Who’s next?” asked Ms. Pickles.

“Zack?”

Zack pulled out a key chain

from his pocket.

“This is Bridget,” he said.

"It's just a dumb key chain!"
said Buster.
He tried to grab Bridget,
but he knocked her
out of Zack's hand.

Bridget landed in the aquarium!

“Now watch this!” said Turk.

Bridget began to grow larger,

and larger, and larger.

“My goodness!”

cried Ms. Pickles.

“Oh,” said Bridget.
“This feels great!”

“Wow!” said Sam. “A crocodile!”

Bridget jumped up.

“I beg your pardon!” she said.

“I am a *gator*,

a gator from the Glades.”

"Where did you get her?"

asked Becky.

"From my uncle Jim," said Zack.

"He lives in the Everglades."

"She is *alive*,"

said Ms. Pickles.

"Does she bite?" asked Becky.

"Sometimes," said Bridget.

"I want one like her!" said Amy.

"Me too," said Becky.

"Hey, Zack!" said Bridget.

"Is this school?"

"Yes," said Zack,

"and these are my friends."

"Pleased to meet you!"

said Bridget.

She began to sing:

"I feel great!

ALLIGATOR great!"

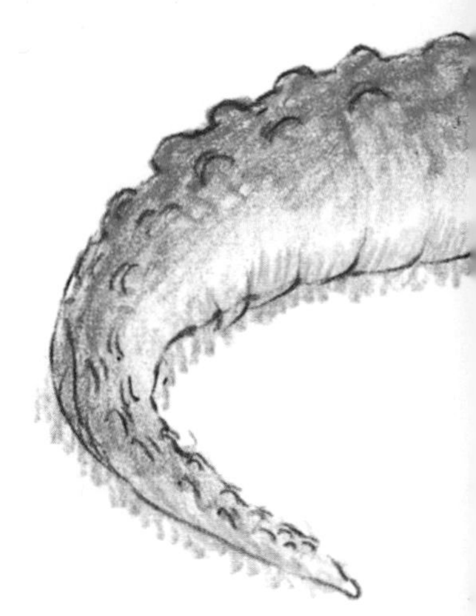

Just then

Buster dropped Negatron.

The robot began to march

across the room.

WHIRRRRRR! WHIRRRRRR! WHIRRRRRR!

"Don't worry!" said Bridget.

"I will get that monster!"

"No!" shouted Buster.

But Bridget did not stop.

“Watch out!” cried Ms. Pickles.

The class moved out of the way.

“Come on, Bridget!” said Turk.

“Where did he go?” cried Bridget.

“Over here,” said Amy.

Bridget grabbed Negatron and said,

"Got you! You won't *whir*

around here anymore!"

Click, buzzz, click, click.

Then Negatron stopped.

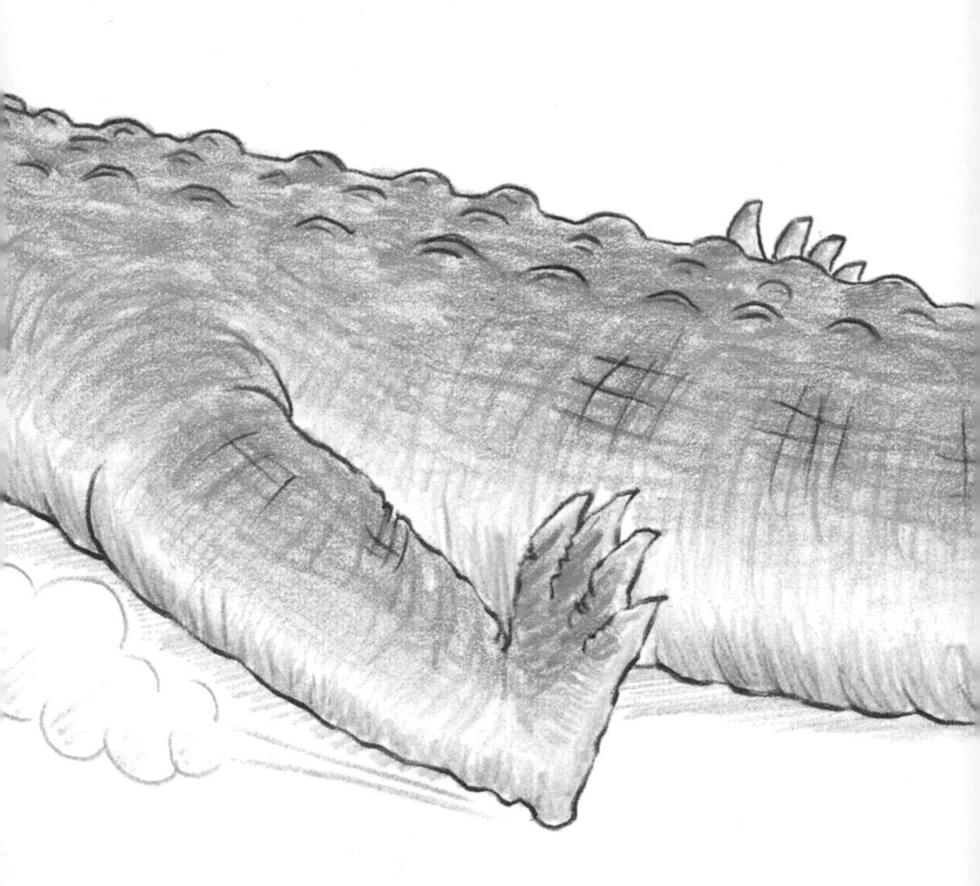

“Give me that,” said Buster.

“What’s the magic word?”

asked Bridget.

"Please," he said.

"I did not want that thing anyway,"

said Bridget.

Suddenly she saw a dinosaur balloon.

“Cousin!” she shouted.

“It’s good to see you!”

As Bridget ran to the dinosaur,

she stepped on Amy's skateboard.

"*Wheeeee!*" she yelled.

"This is fun!"

"Stop!" cried Ms. Pickles.

Bridget went too fast.

Crash!

She knocked over the ant farm

and bumped into the radio.

Ants crawled out.

Music played.

"Ugh!" said Bridget.

"I hate ants,

but I *love* music!"

“This has gone far enough,”

said Ms. Pickles.

“I’m getting the principal!”

Bridget jumped back

on the skateboard.

“Wait!” said Amy. “Put these on.”

Amy helped Bridget put on a helmet, knee pads, and elbow pads.

"There," said Amy.

"Now you are ready."

Bridget skated over to the dinosaur.

“Let’s dance!” she said.

Bridget whirled and twirled

the dinosaur around the room.

“You are so light on your feet!”

she said.

But Bridget whirled and twirled
the dinosaur too hard.
Whooosh!
It flew across the room
and crashed into Buster.

"Oh, no!" cried Bridget.

"What have I done to you?"

"Don't worry," said Becky.

"You just knocked the air

out of him."

Then Bridget saw something else.
"What is this?" she asked.
"It is a map," said Zack.
"Here is where we live,
and here are the Everglades."
"That does not look like home,"
said Bridget.
"It is too small and dry,
and there are no fish or snakes."
Zack said,
"But this is not really—"

Just then Nancy threw
her basketball to Bridget.
"Catch!" she said.

Bridget caught the ball
and threw it back.

"This is fun!" said Bridget,

and she sang:

"I can do anything!

And I mean anything!"

Suddenly Bridget stopped.

"I am thirsty," she said.

Zack gave her some orange juice.

Then Bridget ate Zack's sandwich.

"Meat Loaf Special," she said.

"My favorite!"

Bridget ate all of Zack's lunch,

even the pickles and bananas.

“That was a nice snack,” she said.
Then Turk gave Bridget
his tuna sandwich.
Amy gave Bridget
her peanut butter sandwich.

Even Buster said,
“Here, you can have mine.”
“Delicious!” said Bridget.

"Let's play with my detective set,"

said Turk.

"I can take your footprints.

Press your feet down on this inkpad.

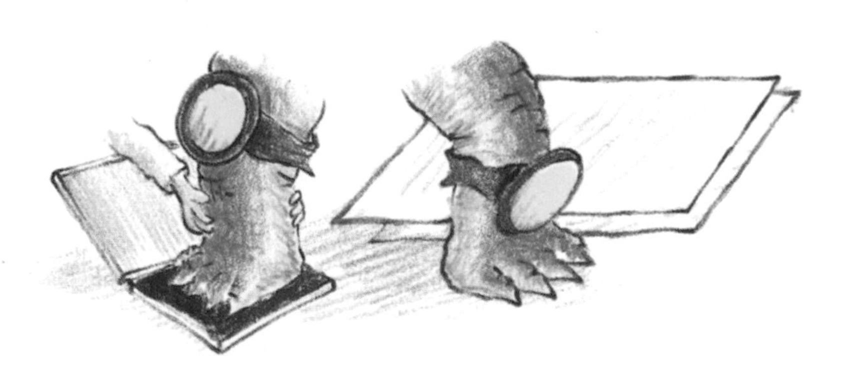

Now press them down on the paper."

When Bridget picked up her feet,

there were two large prints.

"Ooh, this is fun," she said.

“Let’s do my other two feet!

That tickles,” said Bridget.

Now Turk had four prints.
But the last two prints
were smaller.
“She is shrinking,” said Turk.
“I know,” said Zack.

Bridget danced over to Amy's desk and sang:

"Oh I'm a gator from the Glades.

I love snakes and slugs!

I love alligator hugs!"

Bridget was becoming smaller
and smaller, and smaller.
"She needs water,"
said Zack.

Just then Ms. Pickles came back
with the principal, Mr. Turnip.
"What's all this I hear
about an alligator?"
asked Mr. Turnip.
The children ran to their seats.

"Good-bye, Bridget," Amy said softly,
and passed Bridget to Becky.
"May I see that?"
asked Mr. Turnip.

Becky held up Bridget.
"This belongs to Zack,"
said Becky.

"It's only a key chain,

Ms. Pickles," said Mr. Turnip.

"Oh, no, it isn't,"

said Ms. Pickles.

But Mr. Turnip left.

Becky passed Bridget to Buster.

Bridget smiled at Buster,

and Buster smiled back.

He gave Bridget to Turk.

“It’s been fun, Bridget,” Turk said,

and he gave Bridget to Zack.

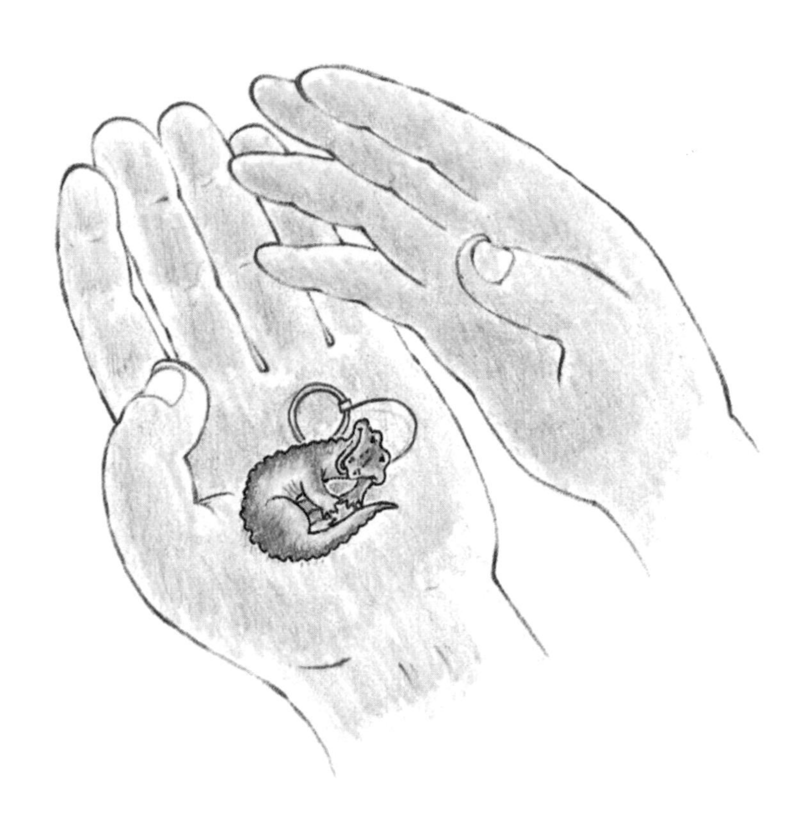

Bridget looked up at Zack.

"I did it all,"

she said.

"Now I am sleepy."

"I know," said Zack. "Sleep tight."

"Will you water me again soon?"

asked Bridget

"Yes," said Zack.

"See you later alligator."

Bridget smiled and went to sleep.